CW01645722

JEFFREY COLE

Timeless Love

A Korean Historical Time Travel Romance

First published by JEFFREY COLE 2025

First edition

This book was professionally typeset on Reedsy.
Find out more at reedsy.com

To those who believe love can defy time—
this story is for you.
And to every soul who once loved in silence,
only to find their voice in a dream.
—Jeffrey Cole

"Even if the stars forget our names
and time erases our footprints—
if our hearts remember,
then we have never truly been lost."

—Unknown

Contents

Foreword

When I first imagined *Timeless Love,* I didn't know I would be swept into a story that spanned centuries, crossing the delicate line between fate and free will. This story is a love letter to every drama that ever made us cry at 2AM, to every reader who has ever wished to time-travel through emotion, and to every dreamer who still believes in a once-in-a-lifetime kind of love.

As you turn these pages, I invite you to lose yourself in a world of ancient palaces, forbidden glances, and love that echoes beyond the reach of time.

—Jeffrey Cole

Preface

Timeless Love began as a simple idea—a modern woman in the wrong era, and a man born centuries too early to love her. But as the story grew, it transformed into something more than just a tale of time travel. It became a story about holding onto love even when the world tries to erase it, about sacrifice, memory, and how destiny always finds a way.

What follows is not just a romance, but a journey. One of tears, longing, and the kind of love that leaves a mark no matter the century.

Acknowledgments

To the readers who have joined me on this journey—thank you for your hearts, your time, and your belief in love stories that bend reality.

To the storytellers of K-Dramas and timeless historical fantasies—you lit the spark that made *Timeless Love* come alive.

To my editor and creative team—your vision polished every word, and your encouragement turned drafts into destiny.

And to time itself—thank you for the what-ifs that inspired this story.

Chapter 1: The Ripple in Time

The rain came in torrents, thick and relentless, drenching the streets of Seoul. Ji-eun darted between umbrellas, clutching her satchel tight against her chest. The museum would close in fifteen minutes, and her professor would surely deduct points if she didn't return the royal seal replica on time.

"Stupid rain," she muttered, her sneakers splashing through puddles.

She dashed into the National Museum of Korean History just as the gates began to close. The security guard gave her a disapproving look, but she bowed politely and scurried past him. The grand hall loomed ahead—dim, quiet, and cavernous. Shadows stretched across ancient artifacts, creating a mysterious aura that made Ji-eun's heart skip.

The seal was part of an exhibition on the Joseon dynasty, where it had been carefully preserved for centuries. Ji-eun was only supposed to borrow the replica for a week for her university thesis, but even the fake object had a weight to it, like it carried centuries of stories.

She returned the seal to the velvet-lined display case with a soft sigh of relief. As she turned to leave, a sudden gust of wind swept through the hall—strange, given the sealed doors and windows. The lights flickered. A low hum filled the air, and the seal began to glow.

Ji-eun blinked. "What the—?"

Before she could take another step, the glow intensified, surrounding her in golden light. Her breath caught. The world blurred, her ears filled with a rushing sound like a thousand whispers in reverse. Her knees gave out, and she fell—

Not onto the polished floor of the museum, but onto grass.

Warm, dew-kissed, and soft beneath her fingers.

She sat up abruptly, her heart racing. The city was gone. In its place stood a dense forest with towering trees and bird calls she'd only heard in documentaries.

"What is this… a dream?"

She tried to stand, but her head swam. When she looked down, she was no longer wearing her hoodie and jeans. Her clothes had transformed into a plain hanbok—simple cotton, cream with a pale blue ribbon.

Footsteps crunched nearby.

Ji-eun froze.

From the trees emerged a group of men in traditional military uniforms—black and red with swords at their sides. Their gazes locked onto her, expressions hardening.

"You there! Identify yourself!" one barked in archaic Korean.

Ji-eun's mouth went dry. "I… I…"

She stumbled over her words, her modern Seoul dialect clashing with the ancient cadence. The men exchanged glances.

"She's dressed like a commoner, but she looks lost," another said. "Could be a spy."

"I'm not a spy!" she cried.

But it was too late. Two of them stepped forward and grabbed her arms. Ji-eun thrashed, panic rising.

"Let go of me! I didn't do anything!"

They hauled her through the woods toward what looked like a palace wall, its gates guarded and high. Ji-eun's mind raced. This couldn't be happening. Time travel? Was she hallucinating? A prank show?

No. This was real. The scent of pine, the weight of the clothes, the bruising grip on her arms—none of it felt fake.

Once inside the compound, she was thrown into a wooden holding room. The door slammed shut.

Alone in the dim space, she curled into a corner, trembling.

Hours passed. She tried to stay calm, piecing together everything she knew. Her thesis was on the royal seal of King Seonjo—a controversial ruler known for both his cunning and cruelty. Had she landed in *his* era?

The door creaked open.

Ji-eun stood instinctively. A man entered—not a guard, but someone of higher status. His robes were of fine silk, dark blue with golden embroidery, and his gaze was piercing.

"Your name," he demanded.

Ji-eun swallowed hard. "Lee Ji-eun."

He raised an eyebrow. "That's a strange name."

"It's... from a far province," she lied.

He stepped closer, studying her like she was a puzzle. "I am Kim Jihan, Minister of Justice. You were found trespassing near the palace. Explain yourself."

Ji-eun tried to keep her story simple. "I got lost in the forest. I don't remember how I got here."

"A commoner with no escort, wandering near the royal grounds?" His tone was skeptical.

"I'm telling the truth."

His eyes flicked over her. "Your accent is strange, your clothes poorly made but unusually stitched. Who sent you?"

"No one!" she insisted. "I don't belong here. I'm not supposed to be here."

His gaze softened for a brief second—just long enough for Ji-eun to glimpse something behind the cold façade. Curiosity? Concern?

Then he turned away. "You'll be sent to the palace court for questioning tomorrow. If you lie, the punishment will be severe."

He left, and the door closed again.

Ji-eun sank to the floor. "This is insane..."

The next day came fast. She was dragged through palace halls teeming with courtiers, ladies-in-waiting, and noblemen whispering behind fans. The opulence stunned her—gilded ceilings, carved dragons, lotus lanterns swaying with every step.

She was brought before a panel of ministers and advisors, presided over by none other than the Crown Prince.

Ji-eun's breath caught when she saw him.

Tall, regal, with a gaze so intense it made her chest tighten. His long dark hair was half-tied, and his robes were white with silver patterns. He looked like he had walked straight out of a historical drama—and her wildest dreams.

"This woman was found trespassing in the forest," Jihan explained. "She claims to have no memory of how she arrived."

The prince looked at Ji-eun. "What is your name?"

"Lee Ji-eun," she replied, heart pounding.

"Where is your home?"

"Seoul."

The courtiers exchanged confused glances.

"Seorul? Do you mean Seorabeol?" someone asked.

Ji-eun fumbled. "Y-yes."

The prince's eyes narrowed slightly, but he said nothing. "Until we determine her origin, she will serve in the palace kitchen under supervision."

Ji-eun gasped. "Wait—what?"

"It is that or imprisonment," the prince said coldly.

She bit her lip. "Fine..."

Thus began Ji-eun's life in the palace—washing vegetables, scrubbing floors, enduring stares and whispers. She tried to stay low, but curiosity always found her.

Especially from one person.

Prince Hyun.

He watched her often, though he pretended not to. When he passed by, her heart stuttered. He was a mystery—stoic but kind, powerful yet restrained. Something about him felt oddly familiar, as if they'd met before.

Late one night, she found herself outside the royal library, unable to sleep. A rustle caught her ear. She peeked inside—and there he was.

Alone, reading by candlelight.

Their eyes met.

"You again," he said quietly.

"I couldn't sleep," she admitted.

He closed his book. "Most servants wouldn't dare enter the royal library."

"I'm not most servants."

He smiled faintly, the first true expression she'd seen on him.

"Where are you really from, Lee Ji-eun?"

She hesitated. "You wouldn't believe me if I told you."

"Try me."

"I'm from the future. The year 2025."

The candle flickered.

Silence stretched between them.

"Interesting story," he said finally. "Are there flying carts in this future?"

Ji-eun laughed softly. "Not yet. But we have phones, electricity, planes..."

"Sounds like magic."

"Sometimes, it feels like it."

He leaned forward, studying her with a new intensity. "Then why are you here?"

"I don't know," she whispered. "I touched a seal, and the next thing I knew—I was here."

His brows furrowed. "A royal seal?"

She nodded.

He leaned back slowly, deep in thought. "There is a legend... about a seal that controls time. My grandfather once spoke of it. Said it disappeared centuries ago."

Ji-eun's eyes widened. "What if I triggered it?"

"Then you were never meant to be here."

A pause.

"Or," he added softly, "perhaps you were."

Their eyes locked in the golden candlelight, a thread of connection tightening between them.

Ji-eun's heart thudded. She didn't know why, but something told her this meeting wasn't by chance. That Prince Hyun... was the key to everything.

And maybe—just maybe—so was she.

Chapter 2: A Forbidden Connection

The days that followed felt like a blur to Ji-eun. The palace, with its labyrinthine halls and towering stone walls, seemed both foreign and oddly familiar. She spent her days in the kitchens, chopping vegetables and kneading dough, her every movement carefully watched by the head cook and other servants. She didn't mind it much—after all, she had no choice. But every glance, every whispered word from the other servants, made her feel like an outsider.

It was the evenings that were the worst.

Every night, she found herself lying awake in the small servant quarters, staring at the ceiling. Thoughts of the prince filled her mind—the way his eyes had softened when they locked during their brief conversation in the library, his enigmatic smile. She wondered if he truly believed her about being from the future, or if he had simply humored her. The more she thought about it, the more she realized how much he intrigued her.

But she couldn't let herself be distracted. She had to find a way back to her own time. The thought of being trapped in the past forever was terrifying. There had to be a way to reverse the effects of the seal, to return to her life in 2025. But how?

The answer, it seemed, was hidden within the very palace walls.

One evening, while cleaning the royal dining hall, Ji-eun overheard a conversation between two high-ranking courtiers. They were speaking in hushed tones, but her sharp ears caught every word.

"The seal is missing," one said. "The royal family's seal. If it doesn't return by the end of the week, there will be consequences."

"The consequences will be dire indeed," the other replied. "The Emperor will not tolerate such a loss. It is said that whoever holds the seal possesses the power to control time itself. Whoever has it now... could change everything."

Ji-eun's heart skipped a beat. The seal—the one she had accidentally touched. Could it be that her arrival in this time was tied to the missing royal seal? Was it truly capable of controlling time? The idea both terrified and fascinated her.

She had to find out more.

The next morning, she resolved to investigate. But her plans were interrupted when she was summoned to the royal court.

"Ji-eun," a servant called, her voice urgent. "You are to report to the Crown Prince's chambers immediately."

Ji-eun's stomach churned. The Crown Prince? Why would he want to see her?

Her legs felt like lead as she made her way through the palace halls, her mind racing with possibilities. Was this about the conversation she'd overheard? Had the prince somehow discovered her secret?

When she finally reached his chambers, she was escorted inside by a guard. Prince Hyun was seated at a desk, his back to her as he examined a scroll. He didn't look up as she entered.

"Ji-eun," he said without turning around. "I've been told that you have knowledge of the seal."

Ji-eun's heart stopped. "What?"

"You've heard of it," he said, turning to face her. His gaze was piercing, intense. "I know you have."

She swallowed hard, her mind whirling. She couldn't lie, not now. Not to him. "I... I don't know much. Just that I... touched it, and... something happened. I was brought here."

He studied her carefully, as if weighing her every word. "You're telling the truth?"

"I swear," she said, feeling her pulse quicken. "I didn't mean to do anything. I just... I don't know why I'm here."

Prince Hyun leaned forward, his expression unreadable. "I believe you. But you must understand, Ji-eun, the seal is not just a symbol of the royal family. It is said to hold power beyond anything we can comprehend. Whoever controls it can change the course of history."

Ji-eun blinked. "You mean... time?"

He nodded. "Yes. Time itself. And if the seal falls into the wrong hands, it could destroy everything. That is why it must be returned. At all costs."

A cold shiver ran down Ji-eun's spine. "But... I didn't take it. I didn't mean to."

Prince Hyun's gaze softened for a moment, and Ji-eun could have sworn she saw a flicker of sympathy in his eyes. "I believe you. But we must find it, and we must find it soon."

Ji-eun's mind raced. The royal seal, the one she had touched—was that the reason she had ended up in this time? And if so, how could she return to the future? How could she undo the damage she had caused?

Prince Hyun's voice broke through her thoughts. "I need your help, Ji-eun. You are the only one who can understand the seal's true power. The others don't know what they're dealing with. But you..."

Her breath caught in her throat. "What do you want me to do?"

"I need you to find the seal," he said, his tone earnest. "And when you do, bring it to me."

Ji-eun's heart pounded in her chest. This was her chance. The chance to return home. But it also meant putting her trust in Prince Hyun, someone she barely knew. Someone who had the power to control everything.

"I'll help you," she said, her voice barely above a whisper. "But... you have to promise me something."

He raised an eyebrow. "What?"

"You have to promise me that if I help you find the seal, you won't use its power to change history. No matter what."

His gaze hardened. "I cannot make that promise. The power of the seal is too great. But I will do everything in my power to keep it safe."

Ji-eun hesitated. She wasn't sure if she trusted him—after all, she barely knew him. But something about his presence, the way he spoke with such conviction, made her believe that he truly meant it.

"I'll help you," she said again, her voice firm. "But only if you swear you'll keep it safe."

He met her gaze, and for a long moment, neither of them spoke. Finally, he nodded.

"I swear it."

Ji-eun exhaled a breath she hadn't realized she was holding. She had made her choice. She was in this now, for better or worse.

"Where do we start?" she asked.

Prince Hyun stood, his eyes dark with determination. "We start with the past."

Chapter 3: The Search Begins

The sun rose over the palace, casting a golden light over the sprawling grounds. The heavy silence of dawn was broken only by the sound of Ji-eun's footsteps as she walked alongside Prince Hyun through the palace gardens. The air was cool, the scent of blooming flowers mixed with the earthy smell of ancient stone. It was beautiful, almost surreal. Yet Ji-eun's mind was consumed with the task ahead.

Finding the royal seal.

How had she ended up in the past? Was it truly the seal's power that had brought her here? And why, out of all the people in this era, was Prince Hyun asking for her help? She had no answers, only a growing sense of dread that she might not be able to return home.

"Ji-eun," Prince Hyun's voice broke through her thoughts. She looked up at him, his profile illuminated by the soft morning light. "You seem lost in thought."

"I am," she admitted. "This is all so much. I don't even know where to begin."

He stopped walking and turned to face her, his expression serious. "I understand. But we don't have time to waste. The seal's power is not something we can ignore. If it falls into the wrong hands..."

He trailed off, his gaze flicking toward the palace walls, his mind clearly elsewhere. Ji-eun felt a pang of unease in her chest. She wanted to trust him, but the weight of the situation felt heavier with every passing minute. The palace, once a symbol of elegance and grandeur, now felt like a prison—its beauty masking the danger that lurked within.

"I don't even know what the seal looks like," Ji-eun confessed. "How am I supposed to find it if I don't know what I'm looking for?"

Prince Hyun's eyes darkened, his lips pressing into a tight line. "That is why we need to find someone who does."

"Someone who knows about the seal?" Ji-eun asked, her curiosity piqued.

He nodded, a flicker of something dangerous crossing his face. "Someone who understands its power. Someone who can help us retrieve it."

"Who is that?"

"A scholar," he replied. "One who has studied the history of the royal family and the legends surrounding the seal. He lives in the mountains to the north, in a secluded temple."

Ji-eun's eyes widened. "A scholar in a temple?"

"Yes. He has been in hiding for years. The royal family banished him after he grew too powerful, too knowledgeable about the ancient secrets of the kingdom."

"Why would he help us?"

"Because he owes me," Prince Hyun said quietly, his voice carrying an edge of something more personal.

Ji-eun didn't press further, but the sudden shift in his demeanor intrigued her. It was as though this scholar was more than just a person of knowledge—he was someone with a deeper connection to the prince.

"Do you think he'll have the answers we need?" she asked.

"I don't know," Hyun admitted. "But it's our only chance. And time is running out."

The urgency in his voice sent a chill down her spine. They didn't have the luxury of time, and the weight of their task pressed heavily on both of them. The royal seal, with its power to control time, was not something to be taken lightly. And if anyone else got their hands on it, the consequences could be disastrous.

"We leave tomorrow," Prince Hyun said. "Prepare yourself."

The thought of leaving the palace, of venturing into the unknown, stirred a mixture of fear and excitement within Ji-eun. She had always dreamed of adventure, of being part of something larger than herself. But this—this felt different. This wasn't some fantasy; this was real, and the stakes were high.

She spent the rest of the day preparing for the journey. She gathered supplies, packed a small bag, and tried to mentally prepare herself for what lay ahead. That night, she could barely sleep, her mind racing with thoughts of the seal and what it could mean for her future.

The following morning, she stood at the gates of the palace, ready to leave. Prince Hyun was already there, his face set in determination. He had changed into traveling clothes—simple but elegant, fitting for a prince who would soon be in the wilderness. His expression was unreadable, as always, but Ji-eun couldn't shake the feeling that he was hiding something.

"Ready?" he asked, his voice soft but firm.

"As ready as I'll ever be," she replied, trying to ignore the flutter in her stomach. There was something about him—something magnetic, like a force pulling her in that she couldn't quite explain.

They mounted their horses and rode out of the palace gates, leaving the safety of the royal grounds behind. The city of Seorabeol soon faded into the distance, replaced by rolling hills and dense forests. The road was rough, and the journey was long, but Ji-eun couldn't help but feel a sense of freedom. For the first time since arriving in this time, she felt like she was in control, taking action rather than being dragged along by fate.

As they rode through the wilderness, Prince Hyun remained mostly silent, his attention focused on the path ahead. Ji-eun, on the other hand, couldn't stop her mind from wandering.

"Why didn't the scholar just come to the palace?" she asked after a while, breaking the silence.

Prince Hyun's expression hardened slightly. "The royal family cannot know of his involvement. If they do, it will be the end of him—and me. That is why we must find him in secret."

Ji-eun nodded, understanding the gravity of the situation. She had no idea what kind of danger they were truly in. She only knew that the deeper they got into this search, the more their lives would be on the line.

As night began to fall, they set up camp near a small stream. Ji-eun helped prepare a simple meal of rice and dried fish, her hands moving mechanically as she tried to process everything. She still couldn't fully grasp what had happened, why she had been brought here, or how she could possibly help Prince Hyun find the seal.

After they ate, they sat by the fire in silence, the crackling of the flames the only sound between them.

Ji-eun was the first to speak. "Do you ever wonder why it's you? Why you're the one who's been chosen to find the seal?"

Hyun looked at her, his eyes glowing in the firelight. "I don't believe in fate, Ji-eun. I believe in actions. I am where I am because of the choices I've made."

"And what about me?" she asked quietly. "Why am I here? I didn't choose this."

"You're here because the seal chose you," he said, his voice low. "And now, we have to make sure it doesn't destroy everything."

His words hung in the air, heavy with meaning. Ji-eun didn't fully understand it, but somehow, she knew that this was only the beginning of something much larger than herself.

And as the fire flickered, casting long shadows around them, Ji-eun felt the weight of their mission settle deep into her chest. There was no turning back now. They were bound together by fate—whether they liked it or not.

Chapter 4: Secrets in the Temple

The journey to the northern mountains was arduous. The dense forests, steep cliffs, and unpredictable weather made every day a challenge. Despite the hardships, Ji-eun couldn't help but feel a sense of exhilaration. There was something about traveling through this ancient land, with Prince Hyun by her side, that filled her with a strange, inexplicable energy. The air felt different here—crisp, pure, untouched by the modern world she had left behind.

Each day, they rode for hours, stopping only when the sun dipped low in the sky. They spoke little, but the silence between them was never uncomfortable. Ji-eun had learned to read Hyun's subtle expressions, the fleeting glances he threw her way. His eyes were always full of intensity, as if he were constantly thinking, analyzing. His focus on the mission was unwavering, but there was something else—an air of mystery that made her want to know more about him.

But it wasn't just his enigmatic nature that captivated her. There was a quiet strength about him, an authority that seemed to command the land itself. Despite his royal blood, there was no arrogance in his demeanor. He was humble in a way that made him seem more... human.

On the third day of their journey, as they neared the temple where the scholar was said to reside, the weather took a turn for the worse. Thick clouds rolled in from the mountains, and the wind began to howl, biting at their skin. The air grew cold, and Ji-eun's breath turned to mist as she exhaled.

"We should find shelter," she suggested, her voice barely audible above the wind. "We're not far from the temple, but it's too dangerous to continue in this storm."

Prince Hyun nodded, his face grim. "You're right. We'll make camp here."

They found a small clearing sheltered by a thicket of trees and set up their camp. The fire crackled as they huddled close to its warmth, the storm outside growing fiercer by the minute. Ji-eun could hear the howling wind and the occasional rumble of thunder. She couldn't help but feel a sense of foreboding. Something about the storm felt unnatural—too sudden, too intense.

As she sat by the fire, lost in her thoughts, she noticed Hyun staring into the flames, his jaw clenched, his expression tense.

"Hyun," she called softly, "are you okay?"

He didn't answer immediately. Instead, he glanced up at her, his gaze piercing. "The storm is not just a coincidence."

Ji-eun frowned, not sure what he meant. "What do you mean?"

"There are forces at work here," he said, his voice low. "Something is watching us. I can feel it."

The hairs on the back of Ji-eun's neck stood up. "You think someone is following us?"

He nodded slowly. "I don't know who or what it is, but we're not alone."

A chill ran through Ji-eun's spine. She had felt a sense of unease ever since they had left the palace, but hearing Hyun's words made it feel all the more real. The idea that someone—or something—was tracking their every move was terrifying.

Just as the silence between them grew heavy, a distant howl echoed through the storm, cutting through the wind. It was unlike any animal sound Ji-eun had ever heard. It was almost human.

"What was that?" she whispered, her voice trembling.

Hyun's eyes narrowed. "Stay close. Whatever it is, it's not friendly."

Ji-eun didn't need to be told twice. She moved closer to Hyun, her heart racing. The fire seemed small and fragile in the face of the storm's fury. Outside, the howl came again, louder this time, and something about it sent a wave of fear crashing over her.

For hours, they stayed alert, eyes scanning the darkness, every shadow seeming to move with a life of its own. The storm raged on, and Ji-eun couldn't shake the feeling that they were being hunted. Her instincts told her that whatever was out there was no mere animal. It was something far more dangerous.

At dawn, the storm began to subside. The howling wind died down, and the sky slowly cleared, revealing a pale, golden light. But Ji-eun knew that the danger wasn't over. Whatever had been tracking them was still out there.

"We need to move quickly," Hyun said, breaking the silence. "The temple is just ahead. We don't have time to waste."

They packed up camp and mounted their horses once more, moving swiftly through the now calm forest. Ji-eun couldn't shake the sense of unease that clung to her. Every rustle of the trees, every snap of a twig beneath their horses' hooves, made her heart race.

Finally, after what felt like an eternity, they arrived at the temple—a large, ancient structure hidden deep in the mountains. The stone walls were covered in moss, and the roof was slanted and worn by years of exposure to the elements. It looked abandoned, forgotten by time.

But Ji-eun could sense the power that lingered in the air. This place was alive with secrets.

They dismounted and approached the entrance, where a set of heavy wooden doors stood ajar. Hyun pushed them open, and they stepped inside.

The interior of the temple was dimly lit, with candles flickering along the walls. The air smelled of incense and age. The stone floors were cold beneath Ji-eun's feet, and the silence was oppressive.

In the center of the room, sitting cross-legged on a large rug, was a man. His hair was long and silver, his robes simple but elegant. His eyes were closed, but Ji-eun could feel the weight of his gaze on them, as if he had known they were coming long before they arrived.

"Prince Hyun," the man said, his voice smooth and deep. "And you must be Ji-eun."

Ji-eun froze. How did he know her name?

Hyun stepped forward, his expression solemn. "Master Lee. We've come for your help."

Master Lee opened his eyes, revealing a pair of dark, almost otherworldly eyes that seemed to pierce straight through Ji-eun. "I know why you've come. The seal has chosen you, Ji-eun. And now, you must learn what it truly means."

Ji-eun's heart raced. The scholar knew about the seal. He knew about everything.

"Please," Hyun said, his voice urgent. "We need your help. The seal has been lost, and if we don't retrieve it soon, everything will be destroyed."

Master Lee nodded slowly, as if he had been expecting this moment for a long time. "I can help you. But first, you must understand what the seal truly is, and what it can do. Only then will you be ready to face the challenges ahead."

He gestured for them to sit, and as they did, he began to speak of the ancient legends—the stories of the royal family, of the seal's creation, and of its unimaginable power. Ji-eun listened intently, her heart pounding with each word.

She was about to learn the truth. And that truth would change everything.

Chapter 5: The Mark of the Past

The candlelight flickered as Master Lee's voice wove a tapestry of forgotten legends. The walls of the temple, etched with age-old carvings, seemed to lean in, listening along with Ji-eun as he spoke.

"Over five centuries ago," Master Lee began, "the royal seal was created not just as a symbol of the king's authority, but as a key to preserving the balance between two worlds—the world of man and the realm of the divine."

Ji-eun leaned forward, her eyes wide. "Two worlds?"

Master Lee nodded. "There exists a rift—an invisible gate hidden within this land—that, if opened, would flood our world with chaos. Only the royal seal can control it. It was imbued with the power of a celestial being... a timekeeper."

Prince Hyun remained silent, but his eyes were focused sharply on Master Lee. Ji-eun glanced at him, wondering how much of this he already knew.

"The timekeeper foresaw that a great disruption would occur," Master Lee continued. "A traveler—not of this era—would arrive to awaken the dormant powers of the seal. That traveler..." His gaze shifted to Ji-eun, "...is you."

Ji-eun's breath hitched. "Me? But I don't understand anything about this place. I don't belong here."

"That is precisely why you do," Master Lee said. "The seal responds to those whose hearts are untainted by the ambitions of this world. It seeks a soul caught between timelines—someone who can see both the past and the future."

Ji-eun's hands trembled in her lap. "But I didn't choose this. I didn't ask to come here."

"The seal chose you, not the other way around," the old man replied gently. "And its choice is never wrong."

Silence fell over them. Ji-eun stared at the temple floor, the weight of her fate pressing heavily on her chest. She had always felt out of place in her own world—never quite belonging, never quite enough. Now, in a time and place she barely understood, she was told she was the key to saving an entire kingdom.

Master Lee stood slowly, moving toward a carved cabinet at the edge of the room. He opened it with reverent hands and retrieved a scroll, bound in black silk. Returning to the center, he carefully unwrapped it, revealing an ancient diagram—a constellation, a symbol, and what appeared to be a series of concentric circles, all radiating from a single central mark.

"The seal was broken into three fragments to prevent misuse," he explained. "One remains at the palace, hidden within the royal archives. The second was lost to history, though I believe it was buried deep within the Forest of Whispers."

"And the third?" Hyun asked, his voice low.

Master Lee looked at Ji-eun. "That one now resides within her."

Ji-eun's heart pounded. "Inside... me?"

"You were marked the moment you crossed into this world. The seal embedded a piece of itself within your soul. That's why you've been having dreams—visions."

Ji-eun's eyes widened. "The vision of the burning palace... the blood on my hands..."

Master Lee nodded solemnly. "It's not just a vision. It's a memory of what's to come—unless the seal is made whole again."

A chill ran down her spine. She had thought the dream was just a manifestation of fear, of being lost in time. But now she realized it was a warning.

"What do we do now?" Prince Hyun asked.

"You must find the second fragment," Master Lee said. "Only with it can you unlock the full memory buried within Ji-eun. And only then can she guide you to the gate."

"And the Forest of Whispers?" Ji-eun asked. "Where is it?"

"It lies beyond the western ridge," he answered. "A cursed forest no one dares enter. But you must. The seal calls to its own. It will guide you... but beware. You are not the only ones seeking it."

A flash of dread crossed Hyun's face. "The Council?"

Master Lee nodded grimly. "They have sent hunters. They believe Ji-eun is a threat to the throne. They will try to capture her—or worse."

Ji-eun felt Hyun's hand brush against hers, so quick and fleeting she almost missed it. But the silent gesture sent warmth through her, a promise without words.

"We'll leave at dawn," Hyun said firmly. "We won't let them get to her."

That night, Ji-eun couldn't sleep. She wandered outside the temple, the crisp mountain air brushing against her skin. The moon hung low in the sky, casting a pale glow over the courtyard.

She stood there, staring up at the stars. So many nights she had looked at this same sky from her apartment in Seoul, never imagining she would one day be looking at it from the past. The thought was surreal, and yet the cold stone beneath her feet was all too real.

Footsteps approached. She didn't need to turn to know it was him.

"I thought you'd be asleep," Prince Hyun said quietly.

"I couldn't," she replied. "Too much in my head."

He stood beside her, silent for a moment. "What Master Lee said... it's a lot to take in."

"Yeah," Ji-eun murmured. "You think he's right? That I'm really the one who has to do all this?"

"I believe the seal wouldn't have chosen you without reason," he said. "And I believe in you."

She looked at him then. For the first time, she saw something deeper in his eyes—something that went beyond duty or loyalty to the crown. It was a fierce protectiveness, tinged with something gentler, something unspoken.

"You barely know me," she whispered.

Hyun's gaze didn't waver. "I know your courage. I've seen your strength. That's enough for me."

The words lodged in her chest like a lump she couldn't swallow. No one had ever looked at her like that before—not in her world.

A soft breeze rustled the leaves above them, and the silence that followed felt sacred.

"Hyun," she said, her voice almost too soft to hear, "what happens if we find the seal and I... go back?"

He looked away, the muscles in his jaw tightening. "Then you'll go back to the life you were meant to live."

"And you?" she asked.

He didn't answer for a long time. Then, finally, he said, "I'll stay here. In a kingdom held together by the threads of fate... and memories of you."

Her heart cracked a little.

The next morning, they set out for the Forest of Whispers. As they descended from the mountains and traveled westward, the landscape grew darker, the trees thicker. Locals they passed on the road made protective signs and warned them not to go further.

"No one who enters that forest returns the same," an old woman told

Ji-eun at a roadside inn. "Some say it steals your memories. Others say it shows you your greatest fear."

As night fell on the edge of the forest, Ji-eun stood before the tangled wall of trees, her heart pounding. The wind whispered through the branches, as if the forest were calling to her.

She turned to Hyun. "Are you ready?"

He stepped beside her, his hand brushing hers again. "With you? Always."

Together, they crossed the threshold, the darkness swallowing them whole.

And somewhere deep within the forest, something ancient stirred—awake, aware, and waiting.

Chapter 6: Whispers in the Dark

The moment Ji-eun stepped into the Forest of Whispers, she felt it—an eerie silence that pressed against her ears, heavy and unnatural. The air was thick with moisture, and the scent of moss and ancient bark clung to every breath. Shadows danced between the trees, though there was no wind. Even the birds seemed to know not to cross the threshold.

Prince Hyun walked beside her, his expression unreadable, but his sword hand never strayed far from the hilt. Ji-eun found comfort in his presence, his calm demeanor a steady beacon in a place where everything felt wrong.

Hours passed as they moved deeper into the forest. The light dimmed despite the midday sun, and the trees grew denser, their gnarled branches twisting like arthritic fingers. Occasionally, Ji-eun thought she saw something—a flicker of white cloth behind a tree, a shadow darting just out of reach—but when she turned, there was nothing.

"The forest plays tricks on the mind," Hyun said quietly, his voice startlingly close.

Ji-eun glanced at him. "You've been here before?"

He shook his head. "No one dares. But the stories… they say the forest feeds on fear, on longing. It gives you what you most desire, but only so it can take it away."

A chill ran down her spine. "That's comforting."

They came to a clearing as the last slivers of daylight filtered through the canopy. The ground was softer here, blanketed in a bed of white petals that seemed untouched by time. In the center stood a large stone pillar, half-buried in ivy. Strange markings were carved into its surface—symbols Ji-eun recognized from Master Lee's scroll.

"This must be it," she whispered, stepping forward. But as her foot crossed the threshold into the clearing, something shifted.

The forest fell completely silent.

Then, everything changed.

Ji-eun blinked—and the world around her dissolved into mist.

When the fog cleared, she found herself standing in the middle of a bustling marketplace—not the eerie forest, but somewhere else entirely. The sun was bright overhead, and people passed by her in hanbok, their laughter ringing in her ears. It was Seoul—but older. Ancient. And somehow... familiar.

"Ji-eun."

She turned.

There he was—Hyun. But not in the prince's clothing she'd come to expect. He wore a scholar's robe, his hair tied in a simple topknot, and his face was alight with joy.

"Come on!" he called, grinning. "We'll miss the play."

She took a hesitant step forward. "Hyun?"

He laughed, the sound warm and carefree. "Who else would it be?"

Confused but drawn to him, she followed. Everything felt so real—the scent of grilled rice cakes, the warmth of the sun, the sound of children playing. And Hyun's hand... when he reached for hers, it felt like home.

But just as she was about to speak again, the sky darkened. The people around her froze mid-step, like marionettes with cut strings. Hyun turned to her, his expression morphing into something she'd never seen before—sorrow.

"Ji-eun," he said, voice echoing unnaturally, "do you remember this day?"

She tried to answer, but her voice caught in her throat.

"This is a memory from your past," he continued, "but not your past in this lifetime."

The world began to dissolve again, but before it did, Ji-eun saw something—blood on the scholar's robe. Hyun, lying in her arms, eyes lifeless. And her own voice crying out through tears, "Don't leave me. Please."

Then everything went black.

Ji-eun gasped awake on the forest floor, her chest heaving. The clearing was gone. The pillar was still there—but now glowing faintly with a pulsing blue light. Prince Hyun knelt beside her, panic etched across his face.

"You were unconscious," he said. "For hours. I couldn't wake you."

Ji-eun sat up, shivering despite the warmth. "I saw... something. A memory. Of us. But not like this. A past life, maybe?"

Hyun's brows furrowed. "Tell me."

She recounted the vision—the marketplace, the play, the way he had smiled, and then the sudden shift, the sorrow, the blood.

When she finished, Hyun was quiet for a long time. "There are legends," he said finally. "Of lovers cursed to find each other in every lifetime, only to be torn apart before their love can last."

Ji-eun's heart ached. "Do you think that's us?"

He didn't answer. But he reached for her hand and held it tightly.

The pillar pulsed again. As Ji-eun approached, the markings glowed brighter. Her hand hovered over the surface, then touched it.

A surge of energy jolted through her, and the world spun again.

This time, she wasn't transported into a vision. Instead, something within her unlocked—a clarity she hadn't known she was missing. A memory not of another life, but from days ago, hidden by time.

She remembered standing on the edge of a cliff the moment the lightning struck the ocean. She'd been running—chased. Not by time or storm, but by men. Soldiers in dark robes. One of them had shouted something: "She has the seal fragment!"

And then—pain. A sharp blow. A flash of light.

Ji-eun staggered back from the pillar.

"I remember," she whispered. "I wasn't brought here by accident. Someone wanted to stop me. They knew I was coming."

Hyun stood, tense. "Who?"

She looked at him, fear returning to her eyes. "The Council. They're not just after the seal. They're trying to manipulate time itself."

Just then, a rustling in the trees made them both freeze.

Hyun drew his sword.

Figures emerged—cloaked in black, faces hidden behind masks. Ji-eun counted five, then seven. Armed. Silent.

"They found us," Hyun growled.

The attackers moved in a circle, surrounding them. Ji-eun's heart pounded as she backed closer to Hyun, who kept his sword steady.

A voice rang out from behind one of the masks. "Hand over the girl."

Hyun stepped forward, sword raised. "You'll have to go through me."

"So be it."

The forest erupted into chaos. Swords clashed. Hyun fought with the grace and precision of a warrior born, but he was outnumbered. Ji-eun backed away, scanning for an escape, when suddenly—one of the attackers lunged at her.

She screamed and raised her arms.

A flash of blue light burst from her hands, throwing the attacker backward as if hit by a wave. The others froze, stunned.

Hyun turned, wide-eyed. "You... what did you do?"

"I don't know," she whispered, staring at her trembling hands. "It just... happened."

The attackers, shaken, began to retreat. "She's awakening," one of them said, panic in their voice. "We weren't told she could do that!"

In moments, they disappeared into the trees.

Ji-eun fell to her knees, breathless. Hyun rushed to her side, gripping her shoulders.

"You're okay," he said. "You're okay."

She shook her head. "I don't understand any of this. Why me? Why now?"

Hyun touched her cheek, his thumb brushing away a tear. "Because time chose you. And I… I choose you too."

Their eyes locked. The forest, for once, was silent in reverence.

Somewhere deeper in the woods, the remaining fragment of the seal pulsed—waiting.

But for this moment, wrapped in the safety of his gaze and the thrum of their joined fates, Ji-eun felt the first spark of hope.

A love written not just in the stars—but across centuries.

Chapter 7: Beneath the Crimson Veil

Ji-eun stood at the edge of the royal garden, the moonlight cascading over the palace walls like liquid silver. Her fingers brushed the petals of a blooming peony, its vibrant red glowing softly under the stars. It had been three days since the encounter in the Forest of Whispers, and the memory of it still lingered like a whisper in her blood—especially the moment Hyun had touched her face, the intensity of his gaze carving itself into her heart.

The palace, however, was anything but calm.

Whispers had begun to circulate—of masked men seen in the eastern forest, of strange lights and magic. Ji-eun had been told to remain hidden, especially now that her power had revealed itself, but the walls of the palace felt like a cage. She needed answers. Not just about her purpose here—but about herself.

"You're restless again."

Hyun's voice startled her, but she didn't turn. She could feel him standing behind her, close but not touching. His presence had become familiar, a strange comfort amidst the chaos.

"I can't stay still when it feels like something's coming," Ji-eun said, her voice soft. "It's like I'm walking toward something I've forgotten… or something that's forgotten me."

Hyun stepped beside her, his eyes on the moonlit sky. "There's something I haven't told you."

Ji-eun turned to him, eyebrows raised.

He hesitated. "Before you came here—there were rumors. A prophecy that the Seal of Time would awaken in human form. That it would return to finish what was left undone a hundred years ago. Most thought it was a myth... until you arrived."

"You think I'm that seal?"

"I know you are," he said. "You felt it, didn't you? That power in the forest. The visions. The memory of me dying in your arms—" He stopped, his throat tightening. "It's all connected."

Ji-eun swallowed, the weight of it settling on her shoulders. "But I don't know how to control it."

"You will. I'll help you."

The sincerity in his voice made her chest ache. Before she could respond, a rustle broke through the night air. A servant girl sprinted toward them, panting.

"Your Highness! Lady Ji-eun!" she cried. "You must come. Now. The Queen Dowager demands your presence."

Ji-eun blinked. "Me?"

The girl nodded. "She says it's urgent. She knows... everything."

Everything.

Ji-eun followed Hyun through the winding palace halls, her heart hammering against her ribs. The Queen Dowager had remained elusive until now—a powerful figure behind the throne. If she knew Ji-eun's secret, everything could fall apart.

When they entered the Queen Dowager's chambers, Ji-eun was struck by the scent of incense and the presence of something ancient. The woman sat like stone, her back straight, eyes sharp despite her age. Behind her, a panel of silk screens painted with dragons seemed to shimmer in the candlelight.

"Leave us," she said, her voice like a blade.

Hyun hesitated. "Grandmother—"

"I said leave us."

He glanced at Ji-eun, reluctant, then bowed and left the room.

Ji-eun stepped forward and bowed deeply. "Your Majesty."

The Queen Dowager studied her. "You're not of this world. But I assume you know that already."

"I... I do."

The woman leaned back. "A century ago, a woman like you appeared in this palace. She was said to be a time-walker. She came bearing the first fragment of the Seal of Time. She fell in love with a prince and was betrayed. The seal shattered, and time unraveled. Now, history repeats itself."

Ji-eun's eyes widened. "You knew her?"

"She was my grandmother," the Queen Dowager said flatly. "And she died because the palace feared what she represented."

Ji-eun's knees weakened. "So I... I'm reliving her fate?"

"Unless you choose differently."

The Queen Dowager stood, walking toward her. "Hyun—my grandson—he walks a dangerous path by protecting you. There are others who believe your presence is a curse. They would kill to keep the seal from reforming."

Ji-eun's breath caught. "And what do you believe?"

The woman's expression softened, only slightly. "I believe fate is not a chain—it is a thread. It can be cut or tied anew. But if you are to survive... you must learn to use what lies within you."

She reached into her sleeve and handed Ji-eun a small scroll.

"This will teach you to control your abilities. But you must keep it hidden. Not even Hyun should see it yet."

Ji-eun took it, bowing deeply. "Thank you."

"Do not thank me. If you fail, we all fall."

Outside, Hyun was waiting. Ji-eun tucked the scroll into her robe and gave him a small nod. "She didn't kill me. That's progress."

He offered a weak smile. “She’s not as cold as she pretends to be.”

As they walked back toward her quarters, Ji-eun paused near the entrance of the courtyard. “Hyun?”

He turned.

“Did you mean what you said? That you’d help me, no matter what?”

He stepped closer, his eyes searching hers. “Every word.”

She exhaled slowly. “Then I need to show you something.”

That night, in the privacy of her chamber, she unrolled the scroll. Strange symbols shimmered across the parchment, glowing faintly. Hyun stood behind her, watching in awe.

As she traced the first line with her finger, a ripple of warmth spread through her palm, traveling up her arm. The symbols rearranged themselves, transforming into a language she could somehow understand.

“They’re instructions,” she murmured. “A way to tap into the seal’s energy.”

She tried the first chant—softly, carefully.

The room darkened. A blue light formed in her chest, flickering like a flame.

Hyun gasped. “Your eyes—they’re glowing.”

The energy built until she couldn’t hold it any longer. It burst from her hands, surrounding the room in a soft cocoon of light. Everything froze—like time itself had halted.

Then, just as suddenly, the light vanished. Ji-eun collapsed to her knees.

Hyun rushed to her. “Are you alright?”

She nodded. “I didn’t know I could do that.”

“You stopped time.”

Ji-eun looked down at her hands. “Just for a second. But it felt… natural.”

“You’re more powerful than you realize,” he said, his voice tinged with awe—and fear.

She looked up at him, breathless. "If I can control this... I can find a way home."

Hyun froze, pain flickering across his face.

"You still want to go back?"

Ji-eun's heart clenched. "I... I don't know. I have people waiting for me. A life."

He stepped back, his expression carefully neutral. "Of course."

She stood, reaching for him. "But that doesn't mean I want to leave *you*."

Hyun looked at her hand for a long moment, then took it. "Whatever happens... we face it together."

Their fingers entwined, and for a moment, everything else fell away.

But just as their lips were about to meet, a loud knock shattered the stillness.

"Prince Hyun! You're needed at the palace gates!"

Hyun cursed under his breath. "What now?"

A guard called out, "A strange traveler has arrived—claims to know Lady Ji-eun. Says he came from the future."

Ji-eun's blood ran cold.

She and Hyun locked eyes.

From the future?

Could it be...?

She rushed past Hyun, heart thudding.

At the gates, surrounded by curious guards and wary nobles, stood a man in modern clothing—dusty, disoriented, but unmistakably out of place. His eyes widened when he saw her.

"Ji-eun?"

She froze.

"Sun-woo?" she whispered.

Her college classmate. Her friend. The man who had disappeared two weeks before *she* had fallen through time.

He stumbled forward. "Thank God. I thought I'd lost you."

Hyun stepped protectively between them. "Who are you?"

"I'm here to bring her back," Sun-woo said. "Before it's too late."

Chapter 8: The Rift Between Worlds

The courtyard buzzed with uneasy tension as Ji-eun stared at Sun-woo, her breath caught somewhere between disbelief and dread. Of all the people who could've followed her through time, it was him—Sun-woo, the classmate who had always sat beside her in lectures, the one who had gone missing two weeks before her own disappearance. She hadn't realized just how much comfort his familiar face would bring—or how much chaos it might unleash.

"Sun-woo…" Her voice trembled as she stepped forward. "How… how are you here?"

He looked dazed, exhausted. His clothes were torn, covered in dirt and dried blood. "I don't know. I was at the library, trying to figure out what happened to you. I touched this… this artifact—one I thought was part of the Goryeo Dynasty collection. The next thing I knew, I woke up in a forest full of soldiers chasing a deer with antlers made of gold."

Hyun narrowed his eyes. "And why are you here now? Why seek Ji-eun?"

Sun-woo glanced at Hyun with an instinctive suspicion. "Because she doesn't belong here. She has a life. A future. I thought… I thought if I could bring her back, we could both return."

Ji-eun stood silently between them, her pulse racing. Everything she had fought to understand, to adapt to, had been upended in a single moment. Sun-woo's presence was like a tether pulling her back to the life she had left behind, but another part of her—the one that had found purpose, power, and connection in this ancient world—resisted.

"Where have you been since arriving?" she asked.

"Hiding," he said. "Surviving. I've been tracking rumors of a woman with strange powers, figuring it had to be you. I bribed a trader to help me reach the capital, then the gates..."

Ji-eun looked at him carefully. "You risked everything to find me?"

He nodded. "You don't remember what I told you that night at the café, before you left?"

She frowned. "We were talking about the thesis..."

Sun-woo exhaled a shaky breath. "I told you I liked you. That I didn't want you to leave. But you thought I was joking."

Her heart sank. "I didn't realize you meant it."

Hyun's expression darkened. He turned away, jaw clenched.

The palace guards exchanged glances, unsure of whether to take Sun-woo as a guest or a threat. Hyun raised a hand. "Take him to the east guest quarters. Treat him well but keep him under watch. I'll inform the King."

"Yes, Your Highness."

As the guards led Sun-woo away, his eyes met Ji-eun's. "We'll talk more, okay? I promise, I'll explain everything."

Ji-eun gave a small nod, then watched him disappear into the shadows of the corridor.

Once they were alone, Hyun's voice came low and taut. "So this is the life you left behind."

Ji-eun turned to him. "I didn't choose this. I didn't choose to fall through time."

"But now you have a choice," he said, his gaze unwavering. "He represents everything you knew. And I... I'm just the prince of a crumbling dynasty with a prophecy hanging over my head."

"Don't do this," she whispered.

Hyun stepped closer, close enough that she could feel the pain in his presence. "Ji-eun... if you go back, will you forget everything that happened here? Will you forget me?"

Tears welled in her eyes. "I don't know. I don't even know if going back is possible."

"But it's what he came for. And if it is possible, he'll take you."

"Would you try to stop me?" she asked, trembling.

He looked away. "No. But I'll fight for you. Not with blades, not with threats. With the truth."

Her breath caught.

"I love you," he said softly, like a confession in the dark. "I've tried not to, but I do."

Ji-eun's heart cracked open at the edges.

He continued, "Whatever your past holds, whatever future you think you're meant to return to... I want to be part of your present."

Before she could respond, a shadow appeared at the edge of the corridor. Lady Sook, the palace spy who had once threatened Ji-eun, now bowed with unexpected urgency.

"Forgive the interruption," she said. "But there's been an incident."

"What kind of incident?" Hyun asked sharply.

"An explosion at the western temple. And someone left this."

She held out a cloth bundle. Inside was a charred scroll—a match to the one the Queen Dowager had given Ji-eun.

Ji-eun gasped. "How did they get this?"

Sook's face was grim. "Someone knows what you are, Lady Ji-eun. And they're trying to stop the seal from reforming."

Hyun took the scroll, his expression darkening. "There's a traitor inside the palace."

Sook nodded. "I have suspects, but no proof."

Ji-eun felt the burn of unease in her chest. She had barely begun to understand her power—how could she protect it if others were already moving against her?

That night, Ji-eun couldn't sleep.

Sun-woo's arrival stirred memories of home—her mother's morning phone calls, the ramen shop she passed every day, the neon lights of Seoul that blinked through her dreams. But now, those memories clashed with Hyun's confession, the Queen Dowager's warnings, and the quiet longing that wrapped around her soul when she thought of him.

In the moonlit courtyard, she found Sun-woo sitting beneath a stone lantern, staring up at the stars.

"Can't sleep either?" she asked.

He smiled faintly. "Too many questions."

She sat beside him.

"You've changed," he said, glancing at her. "You're stronger. Calmer. It's like you... belong here."

She hugged her knees to her chest. "Sometimes I wonder if this is where I was meant to be all along."

"I used to believe in fate," he said. "But now I think maybe time is just a test. A chance to figure out who we really are."

She looked at him. "Why did you really come after me?"

He hesitated. "Because I was afraid I'd never get another chance. I liked you for a long time, Ji-eun. I wanted to tell you back in college, but you were always so focused. Then you vanished. I thought—I thought I'd lost you before ever really having you."

She reached for his hand, squeezing it gently. "I'm sorry. I never knew."

His fingers curled around hers. "You still have time to come back. There's a way—I think we can use the seal's energy. I've seen something. A gateway."

Her eyes widened. "Where?"

"In the mountains. It's guarded. But it's real. I think it's how we both got pulled in."

Ji-eun's heart raced. A way home. But to leave... would mean leaving Hyun. Leaving the life she had started to build. And maybe—maybe even changing the past forever.

The next morning, the palace was shaken by more grim news.

The Crown Prince had collapsed.

Poison.

The Queen Dowager called an emergency council meeting, and Ji-eun stood beside Hyun as the royal physicians tried to stabilize the prince.

"He's barely breathing," one of them muttered. "This wasn't meant to kill immediately. It's a warning."

The Queen Dowager turned to Hyun. "You must take his place. Until he recovers, you are the acting Crown Prince."

Hyun stiffened. "Grandmother..."

"It's time," she said firmly. "The kingdom must see strength. And Ji-eun—"

Ji-eun straightened. "Yes, Your Majesty?"

"You must begin your training in earnest. The seal's power is growing. If you wish to survive what's coming, you'll need more than love. You'll need control."

Ji-eun nodded, her heart heavy with decision after decision.

That night, standing between two worlds—one calling her home, the other offering her destiny—she made a vow.

She would master the seal.

She would uncover the truth.

And when the time came to choose between the past and the future... she would follow her heart.

Even if it meant breaking it.

Chapter 9: The Guardian of the Seal

The training grounds deep within the palace were unlike any Ji-eun had ever seen. Walled off from the rest of the world by high stone barriers and guarded by ancient wards etched into the surrounding earth, it was a place of secrets, purposefully hidden from the eyes of courtiers and commoners alike.

She stood beneath the arch of a twisted pine tree, her breath visible in the morning air. The Queen Dowager had summoned someone—a guardian, she had said. Someone who had once trained those born under the curse of the seal, those touched by time.

When Ji-eun saw the woman approaching, she wasn't what she expected.

She was tall, her silver hair tied in a long braid down her back, her eyes sharp and fox-like. She wore the robes of neither court nor temple, but a mixture of both—gray and crimson, symbols of power embroidered subtly into the hem. In her hand was a carved wooden staff, humming softly as it struck the stone with each step.

"You must be the traveler," she said, her voice calm but commanding.

Ji-eun bowed deeply. "Yes. My name is Ji-eun."

"I know who you are. I am Hye-seo, Guardian of the Seal. And if you wish to survive, you will do exactly as I say."

Without another word, she spun and walked toward the inner courtyard.

Ji-eun followed, heart pounding. Every part of her screamed with nerves, but deep inside was a pull—something ancient and buried—that urged her forward.

"You were chosen, not by accident, but by force," Hye-seo said. "Someone broke the boundaries of time to bring you here. That means someone else can do it again. If you remain weak, you are a liability to everyone you care about."

Ji-eun clenched her fists. "Then teach me."

Hye-seo studied her. "You will not like my methods."

"I don't need to like them. I need to learn."

For days, Ji-eun trained. The sessions were brutal—physical, spiritual, and mental. She learned to channel her energy through the seal mark that had begun to shimmer more frequently on her wrist. Hye-seo taught her to feel the threads of time like strings in a web, to recognize the moments where fate tugged hardest.

Some nights, she couldn't even make it back to her quarters, collapsing on the floor of the training hall, sweat soaking her tunic, breath shallow.

But she didn't stop.

Meanwhile, palace life shifted.

With the Crown Prince still unconscious, Hyun began taking on his brother's responsibilities. He presided over court meetings, addressed visiting envoys, and made key decisions that earned both praise and hidden resentment.

Though he wore the royal robes with effortless grace, Ji-eun could see the weight behind his eyes every time he returned from a long day of politics. The boy who had once slipped out of the palace walls with her now looked more like a man destined for war.

Late one evening, as the moon spilled silver across the courtyard, Ji-eun found him standing alone beneath the plum blossom tree.

"Hyun," she said softly.

He turned. "You've barely had a moment to rest. Hye-seo is relentless."

"She has to be," Ji-eun replied. "I don't want to be a pawn anymore."

He smiled faintly. "You were never a pawn. You were the storm that changed everything."

She stepped closer. "You're handling things well. The ministers respect you."

"They respect my title," he said. "Not me. They're waiting for me to fail."

"You won't." Her hand brushed his. "Because you don't stand alone."

His fingers curled around hers, and for a moment, their world shrank to just the space between them.

"I'm afraid," he whispered. "Of losing you."

She swallowed the lump in her throat. "I'm afraid too."

But there was no time to dwell in sweetness. The days grew tenser. Whispers of rebellion grew louder. Someone had poisoned the Crown Prince, and the investigation was stalling. Ji-eun began noticing odd things—courtiers who stared too long, scrolls disappearing from the royal library, Sun-woo being questioned more than once.

She found him one afternoon in the secluded garden, sketching in a notebook.

"Have you seen anything suspicious?" she asked.

Sun-woo looked up. "Aside from half the court acting like they want to burn me at the stake?"

She smiled. "Aside from that."

"I think someone's watching me," he admitted. "I've caught shadows moving behind me. I tried to follow one the other night, but whoever it was disappeared near the northern wall."

Ji-eun frowned. "The same wall where the Queen Dowager told me the first portal appeared centuries ago."

Sun-woo nodded. "It's not a coincidence. Someone wants access to the seal's power."

"And they're getting bolder," Ji-eun muttered. "Hye-seo told me the seal can be used to reopen gateways—but it requires balance. Without it, tearing time open could destroy both worlds."

Sun-woo closed his notebook. "Then we need to stop them before they try."

That night, Hye-seo summoned Ji-eun again—not to train, but to warn.

"I felt something shift," the guardian said. "The seal pulses. That means someone is trying to activate a gate."

Ji-eun's heart raced. "Where?"

"The cliffs beyond the eastern forest. An ancient altar lies buried there—one meant for warlocks, not seers. If they succeed in corrupting the seal's energy, they'll create a rift that could collapse both timelines."

"Then I need to stop them," Ji-eun said.

Hye-seo hesitated. "You are not yet ready."

"I can't wait until I'm ready. I have to go now."

That same night, Ji-eun, Hyun, and Sun-woo rode out under the cover of darkness.

They moved swiftly through the forest, every step leading them closer to the edge of history. When they reached the cliffside, the ground trembled beneath them. Lightning cracked through a sky with no clouds.

At the center of the altar stood a cloaked figure. Around him were four others, their hands raised in invocation.

"Stop!" Ji-eun shouted.

But it was too late.

A blast of energy tore through the cliff, ripping open the sky. A swirling vortex appeared—half shadow, half light—its howl a deafening roar.

The cloaked man turned, and Ji-eun's breath caught.

It was Minister Yoon—the same man who had always whispered in the ears of the elders, the one who had quietly opposed her presence in court.

"You meddle with forces you don't understand," he said. "Time must be corrected."

"This isn't correction," Hyun snarled. "It's destruction."

Yoon sneered. "You were never meant to rule. And she—" he pointed at Ji-eun "—was never meant to exist."

Ji-eun stepped forward, the seal on her wrist glowing. "You're wrong. I was meant to change everything."

Light exploded from her hand as she activated the seal's energy. It surged across the altar, shattering the stones and breaking the invocation circle. The vortex screamed as it began to collapse in on itself.

Yoon shouted in fury. "You fool! You've doomed us all!"

"No," Ji-eun said. "I've just rewritten fate."

With a final burst of light, the rift closed, pulling Yoon and his followers into a void that sealed itself behind them.

Silence fell over the cliff.

Sun-woo dropped to his knees, stunned. "You did it..."

Hyun reached for her, steadying her as she swayed. "Ji-eun, are you alright?"

She nodded weakly. "Just... drained."

As dawn broke over the horizon, painting the sky in hues of gold and fire, Ji-eun realized something vital.

She was no longer the girl who had stumbled into history by accident.

She was part of it now.

And whether she returned to the future or remained in the past... she was ready to decide on her own terms.

Chapter 10: The Heart of Time

Ji-eun awoke in the palace infirmary, her body heavy with exhaustion. She could still feel the crackling energy from the seal, the pull of time twisting and colliding as if she had torn open the very fabric of the universe. It had felt like an eternity, and yet, no time had passed at all.

The events of the previous night were a blur, but the aftermath was unmistakable. The rift in the sky, the battle at the altar, and the confrontation with Minister Yoon. They had stopped him, but at what cost? She felt it in her bones—something had changed. The threads of fate had been pulled, and not just for her.

As she tried to sit up, a soft voice called out, stopping her. "Rest."

Ji-eun turned to see Hyun standing in the doorway, his face a mask of concern. He had changed from his royal garb into something simpler—still noble, but more human in his wear.

"You've been unconscious for two days," he said, stepping closer. "You pushed yourself too hard."

"I had to," Ji-eun replied quietly. "If I hadn't stopped them—"

"You did," he interrupted. "But now, the consequences of that action are on us both."

Her heart sank. "What do you mean?"

Hyun sat beside her, his gaze intense. "The rift you closed wasn't just a tear in time. It was a breach in the balance between the past and future.

And now... the palace is feeling the shift."

Ji-eun frowned. "What shift?"

"The ministers are already whispering that something is wrong," he said. "The power structure is beginning to unravel. And worse—there are rumors of strange phenomena spreading through the kingdom. Unnatural storms, people vanishing without a trace. Something darker has been awakened by your actions."

Ji-eun's stomach churned. She had thought stopping the rift would solve everything. But instead, it seemed as though she had only made things worse.

"I didn't mean to—" she began, but Hyun stopped her with a touch to her hand.

"I know," he said softly. "None of this is your fault."

But it didn't change the reality. The time they had bought by sealing the rift was fleeting. They were running out of time to fix what had been broken.

"I need to speak with Hye-seo," Ji-eun said suddenly, pushing herself to stand.

Hyun caught her arm, his grip firm. "It's not safe to move around just yet. You're still recovering."

"I can't wait any longer," Ji-eun insisted. "If we don't find a way to fix this... everything will fall apart."

Hyun's eyes softened, but his voice remained urgent. "Then let me go with you."

She shook her head. "No. I need to face this alone."

He didn't argue, though his eyes held a quiet worry. "Be careful."

As Ji-eun made her way through the corridors, the weight of the palace seemed to press down on her. The air was thick with tension, as if the walls themselves were holding their breath. It wasn't just the political unrest that worried her—it was something deeper. The seal, the rift, her connection to this time... it all felt like a storm that was gathering strength, and she was at its center.

She finally reached the hidden chambers beneath the palace where Hye-seo resided, her footsteps echoing in the cold stone hallways. The guardian was waiting for her, as if she had expected this visit all along.

"You're here," Hye-seo said, her voice calm but her eyes sharp. "I felt the change."

Ji-eun nodded, her chest tight. "Something is wrong. The rift didn't just close it... it caused a ripple. I can feel it. Something dark is spreading."

Hye-seo motioned for her to sit. "The rift you sealed wasn't merely a doorway. It was a key to a deeper force—something ancient, something tied to the very core of the seal's power."

"What do you mean?" Ji-eun asked, her voice barely above a whisper.

"Long ago," Hye-seo began, "there were those who tried to harness the power of the seal. They wanted to control time itself. But they failed. In their arrogance, they tore apart the balance of time and space, leaving behind remnants of their power. Those remnants have been dormant, waiting for someone to awaken them."

Ji-eun's heart hammered in her chest. "You're saying... I've awakened something?"

Hye-seo nodded. "Yes. The rift you closed—it didn't just seal a tear in time. It triggered the release of the remnants. And now they're stirring."

"Who... who is behind this?" Ji-eun asked, desperation creeping into her voice.

"Minister Yoon," Hye-seo said flatly. "He was only a pawn. The true power behind this movement is someone much older, much more dangerous."

"Who?"

"A being known as the Keeper of Time," Hye-seo replied. "It's said that they are the ones who first bound time itself. They've been hidden, lost to history, but now they've found a way to return."

Ji-eun's mind raced. "What do they want?"

"They want to rewrite time," Hye-seo said. "They want to undo the past and control the future. They believe the seal is the only way to do that."

"But why me?" Ji-eun asked, her voice trembling. "Why is it always me?"

Hye-seo's eyes softened, as if she saw the weight of the question in Ji-eun's soul. "You are the chosen one, Ji-eun. The one whose fate is tied to the seal. You are the key to either saving or destroying this world."

Ji-eun's mind spun. She had never asked for this. She had never wanted any of it. But now, the future of two worlds rested on her shoulders.

"I don't know how to stop them," Ji-eun whispered.

"You must learn," Hye-seo said, standing. "You must find the Heart of Time."

"The Heart of Time?" Ji-eun repeated.

"It is the source of the seal's power. If you can reach it before the Keeper does, you can destroy their ability to rewrite history. But it won't be easy. The Heart is hidden, protected by trials that test your very soul. And even if you find it, the Keeper will stop at nothing to take it."

Ji-eun felt a chill run through her. "Where do I find it?"

"In the mountains to the north," Hye-seo said, her voice low. "There, you will find the first trial. But be warned—it is not only your body that will be tested. It is your heart."

Ji-eun stood, a sense of resolve settling over her. "Then I'll go. I have no choice."

Hye-seo nodded. "I'll help you prepare, but remember—time is a living thing. It will fight back against you. And so will the Keeper."

Ji-eun turned toward the door. "I'll face whatever it takes."

As she walked back to the palace, the weight of Hye-seo's words hung over her. The Keeper of Time. The Heart of Time. Trials of the soul.

It was all too much, but in her heart, she knew one thing for sure: she could not fail. Not for herself, and not for Hyun.

She would find the Heart of Time.

And she would destroy the Keeper's plan before it could unravel everything.

Chapter 11: The Path of Trials

The sun had barely risen when Ji-eun left the palace gates, her heart heavy with the weight of the journey ahead. She had never been more certain of one thing in her life: she could not afford to fail. The Heart of Time awaited her in the northern mountains, and only by finding it could she hope to stop the Keeper of Time and undo the damage caused by her accidental meddling in history.

Her mind raced as she rode through the forest, the cool morning air brushing against her face. Every step took her further away from the safety of the palace, from Hyun, from everything she had known since arriving in this strange era. It felt as if the world around her was shifting beneath her feet, bending to forces she had yet to fully comprehend.

As she traveled deeper into the wilderness, Ji-eun's thoughts turned to Hyun. The way his gaze had lingered on her before she left, the unspoken worry in his eyes. She could feel the bond between them, a connection that transcended time, yet the distance between them now felt like an insurmountable chasm.

She couldn't shake the feeling that time was running out for both of them.

Her journey took her through dense forests, across rushing rivers, and over rocky hills. The landscape grew harsher with each passing day, the mountains in the distance looming like silent giants. Every step forward felt like a battle against her own exhaustion, but she couldn't stop. The fate of two worlds rested on her shoulders.

By the third day, she reached the base of the northern mountains. The towering peaks were covered in a blanket of snow, and a biting wind swept through the valleys, cutting through her thin cloak. Her breath formed clouds of vapor in the air as she stared up at the imposing path ahead.

The first trial awaited her here, Hye-seo had said. And while Ji-eun had prepared herself for physical challenges, she had no idea what lay in store for her.

She stepped forward, her boots crunching in the snow, and the moment her foot touched the mountain's path, she felt a shift in the air—an invisible barrier had been breached. The ground beneath her feet rumbled, and an ethereal light flickered in the distance.

It wasn't long before she saw them—figures cloaked in shadow, emerging from the mist like apparitions. They were tall, their faces obscured by hoods, but their eyes gleamed with an unnatural light. They were the Guardians of the Mountain, ancient beings tasked with protecting the trials that lay beyond.

"You seek the Heart of Time," one of the figures spoke, his voice low and haunting.

"I do," Ji-eun replied, her voice steady despite the dread curling in her chest. "I must pass the trials."

"The trials are not for the weak-hearted," the figure said. "You must prove yourself worthy. Only those who understand the depths of their soul may reach the Heart."

Ji-eun nodded, a fierce determination settling in her chest. "I'm ready."

Without another word, the Guardians stepped aside, revealing the narrow path that twisted upward toward the heart of the mountains. The journey was long, and the trials began almost immediately.

The first trial was a test of strength.

Ji-eun found herself in a wide cavern, surrounded by towering stone walls. The temperature dropped, and a low rumble echoed through the space. Suddenly, the ground beneath her feet cracked open, and from the depths, a massive creature emerged—a serpent-like beast with scales that glimmered in the dim light.

It hissed as it coiled around the cavern, its eyes glowing with malice. Ji-eun's heart raced. She had fought off bandits and wild animals in the past, but nothing like this.

The creature lunged toward her, its jaws snapping. Instinctively, Ji-eun drew a dagger from her side and rushed forward, dodging the creature's strike. She barely avoided its venomous fangs, but she couldn't keep up this game of cat and mouse forever. Her energy was waning, and the creature seemed to grow stronger with each passing moment.

She needed to think fast.

Her hand went to the seal on her wrist, the one that had once felt like an insignificant mark but now pulsed with a strange, powerful energy. As she focused, the seal shimmered, and she felt the familiar pull of time, the way it twisted and moved beneath her fingers.

The serpent lunged again, but this time Ji-eun raised her hand, and with a burst of energy, the beast froze mid-air. Time slowed, the world around her becoming still as she focused all her energy on the creature. With a swift motion, she drove her dagger deep into its heart, ending its reign of terror.

As the serpent's body dissolved into mist, the cavern around her began to shift. The temperature warmed, and the walls crumbled away, revealing the next part of the trial.

Ji-eun barely had time to catch her breath before the second trial began.

She found herself in a dense forest, the air thick with fog. The trees were ancient, their gnarled branches reaching out like twisted hands. As she ventured deeper into the woods, she felt a strange sense of unease—a presence watching her, lurking just beyond the trees.

Suddenly, the mist parted, and she came face to face with her own reflection—a perfect replica of herself, standing tall and unyielding in front of her. The doppelgänger's eyes were cold, unfeeling, and filled with an intensity that mirrored her own.

"You are not ready," the reflection said, its voice eerily similar to her own.

"I am," Ji-eun replied, her voice shaking slightly but growing stronger with each passing moment. "I have to be."

The reflection stepped forward. "You think you can save the world, but you cannot even save yourself."

Ji-eun's heart thudded in her chest as her reflection raised a blade, its edge gleaming in the dim light. "You cannot escape your destiny. It is written."

"No," Ji-eun whispered, the words feeling foreign and yet strangely familiar. "I am not bound by fate."

With a fierce cry, she lunged at her reflection, her blade meeting its twin in a clash of steel. The two figures fought, mirroring each other's every move. But Ji-eun could feel the truth in her heart, something she had never truly understood before. She was not a pawn in someone else's game. She was the master of her own fate.

With a final thrust, Ji-eun pierced her reflection's heart, shattering the illusion. As her doppelgänger vanished, the forest around her faded, leaving behind only the silent whispers of the wind.

She had passed the second trial.

Exhausted but resolute, Ji-eun continued her ascent up the mountain. She had faced the trials of strength and of self, but she knew the hardest test was still ahead of her.

The third and final trial would test her heart.

And as the wind howled through the mountain pass, Ji-eun could feel the pull of destiny drawing her closer to the Heart of Time.

But would she be ready for what awaited her there?

Chapter 12: The Heart of Time

The wind was sharper now, biting through Ji-eun's cloak as she climbed higher into the mountains. Her body was sore from the trials she had already faced—the serpent, the reflection—but her spirit remained unbroken. She had no choice but to keep going. The final trial awaited her, and she could feel the weight of it pressing down on her.

The path narrowed as she approached the summit, the snow now knee-deep. But despite the harsh conditions, a strange warmth began to fill the air, as though she were being drawn into a world beyond the physical. The stone beneath her feet began to glow faintly, casting an ethereal light around her.

She reached a clearing, and there, standing before her, was a massive stone door, its surface inscribed with ancient symbols that shimmered with a pale, otherworldly glow. It was the entrance to the Heart of Time, the source of all power—the key to saving both the past and the future.

Her heart raced as she stepped closer. The door opened silently, revealing a chamber filled with swirling lights. At the center of the room was an altar, and atop it rested the Heart—a glowing orb of pure, radiant energy. It pulsed with life, and Ji-eun could feel its power radiating outward, calling to her.

But as her fingers brushed the door, a voice echoed through the chamber, stopping her in her tracks.

"You think you can control time?" The voice was low and gravelly, filled with ancient wisdom. It seemed to come from everywhere, from the very walls themselves.

Ji-eun's pulse quickened, and she turned to see a figure step out from the shadows. Tall, cloaked in darkness, with eyes that glimmered like starlight. It was the Keeper of Time, the very being she had come to stop.

"You are too late," the Keeper said, his voice like the winds of eternity. "I have waited centuries for this moment. The Heart of Time belongs to me."

Ji-eun's breath caught in her throat. The Keeper of Time was more than just a shadow of the past. He was a force—a being who had existed far longer than any mortal. He had the power to reshape the world, to rewrite history, and now he stood before her, an obstacle she could not easily defeat.

"I won't let you have it," Ji-eun said, her voice trembling but resolute. "I won't let you change everything."

The Keeper laughed, a sound that sent chills down her spine. "You are naïve, child. You cannot stop time. Time is inevitable. It will consume everything."

"I'll stop you," Ji-eun said, stepping forward, her resolve hardening. "I'll use the Heart to stop you."

The Keeper's eyes glinted with amusement. "You think the Heart of Time can be controlled by a mortal like you? You are nothing but a fragment of time yourself. You are a ripple in the grand tapestry. Do you truly believe you can control it?"

Ji-eun didn't respond. She knew what he said was true. She was nothing more than a fleeting moment, a blip in the endless stretch of time. But she also knew that she could not let the Keeper rewrite history. She couldn't let him destroy everything—everything she had fought for, everything she had come to love.

With a deep breath, Ji-eun reached out to touch the Heart. The moment her fingers brushed the glowing orb, the world around her exploded in light.

Time itself seemed to freeze.

The Heart pulsed beneath her fingertips, and she could feel its power coursing through her—faster than she could control, faster than she could understand. It was as if the universe itself was bending, warping, and she was caught in the center of it all. The Keeper's voice echoed in her mind, a warning, a plea, but she could no longer hear it. She could only feel the rush of time.

Memories flashed before her eyes—her life, her journey, her love for Hyun, everything she had experienced. But they were all distorted, twisted into something else, something darker.

She felt herself being torn apart. The very fabric of her existence was unraveling, as though time itself were pulling her in every direction at once.

"No!" Ji-eun screamed, her voice breaking through the chaos. "I won't let you have this!"

With a surge of will, she focused on the Heart, pushing back against the tidal wave of power. Slowly, with great effort, she began to pull herself free. She could feel the Heart's energy pushing against her, but she held on, unwilling to let go.

And then, everything stopped.

The light dimmed. The room went silent. Time, once fractured and chaotic, now settled into a calm stillness.

Ji-eun stood at the altar, her body trembling, her heart racing. She had done it. She had seized control of the Heart of Time. But she knew that this was only the beginning. The Keeper of Time was still there, watching her, waiting for her to fail.

The Keeper stepped forward, his face now visible beneath his hood. His expression was unreadable, but there was something in his eyes—

something dark, something ancient.

"You think you have won," he said softly, his voice no longer filled with the arrogance it had once held. "But the Heart of Time is not a tool for mortals. It is a weapon, one that will destroy you if you are not careful."

Ji-eun's gaze never wavered. "I am not afraid."

The Keeper's lips curved into a faint smile. "You should be."

And with that, he vanished into the air, leaving her standing alone in the chamber with the Heart of Time.

For a long moment, Ji-eun stood there, her fingers still resting lightly on the orb. The world was quiet, still, as if waiting for her to make the next move. Her chest heaved as she struggled to catch her breath, the weight of everything she had just experienced settling heavily upon her shoulders.

But she knew what had to be done. The Keeper of Time may have been defeated, but the battle was far from over. The Heart of Time was still a force to be reckoned with, and Ji-eun had no idea what the future would hold.

But she was ready.

She would face whatever came next.

For Hyun. For herself. And for the world that hung in the balance.

Chapter 13: The Price of Power

The journey back to the palace was quiet, but Ji-eun felt the weight of the world upon her. The Heart of Time pulsed softly in her hand, its glow faint but steady, as though it were alive, waiting for her next move. It was both a comfort and a burden—an object of unimaginable power, yet a reminder of the peril she now faced.

Her thoughts returned to the Keeper of Time, his warning echoing in her mind. The Heart was not meant for mortals, he had said. It was a weapon, and she was playing with fire by wielding it.

But Ji-eun had no choice. She had come too far to turn back now. The fate of both the past and the future rested on her shoulders, and she would do whatever it took to protect them. Even if it meant risking everything.

As she approached the palace gates, the familiar sight of the towering walls brought no comfort. The air felt heavier here, as if something had shifted in the world. She knew that her return would not go unnoticed—especially by Hyun. The love they had shared, the bond that transcended time, was not something that could easily be ignored.

She entered the palace, her heart pounding as she made her way to the private chambers. The halls were eerily quiet, the usual sounds of courtiers and servants muted, as if the palace itself was holding its breath.

She hadn't been back long before she was met with an unexpected presence.

"Ji-eun," a voice called from the shadows. It was Hyun.

She turned to find him standing in the doorway, his expression a mixture of concern and something deeper, something more intense than she had ever seen before.

"Hyun," she whispered, her heart aching at the sight of him. He had been waiting for her, no doubt worried about what had happened. But the moment she saw him, the weight of the trials, of everything she had faced, seemed to lift just a little.

But there was no time for sweet reunions, no time to bask in the warmth of their love. The Heart of Time was still in her hand, and it was pulsing with a strange energy that she couldn't ignore.

"What happened?" Hyun asked, his voice low. "You've been gone for so long, and... you look different."

Ji-eun hesitated, unsure how much to say. She wanted to tell him everything—about the trials, about the Keeper, about the Heart. But there was a part of her that feared he would not understand, that he would try to protect her from the power she now possessed.

"I've done what I needed to do," she said, her voice steady but lacking the usual conviction. "I have the Heart of Time."

Hyun's eyes widened, and for a brief moment, Ji-eun saw fear flicker across his face. He had known what she was going up against, but this was different. The Heart of Time was something beyond their comprehension, something that neither of them fully understood.

"Ji-eun," Hyun began, his voice filled with urgency. "The Heart is not something you can control. You don't know what you're dealing with. The Keeper of Time—he—"

"I know," Ji-eun interrupted, her voice stronger now, though still tinged with uncertainty. "But I couldn't let him have it. I had to stop him. He would have destroyed everything."

Hyun took a step forward, his eyes never leaving hers. "And what about you? What happens to you now? What happens to us?"

Ji-eun's heart clenched at the question. What would happen to them? She didn't have an answer. All she knew was that the Heart was still in her hand, and it was changing her. She could feel the power pulsing within her, twisting and warping her sense of self, as though it were altering her very essence.

"I don't know," Ji-eun admitted softly, her voice breaking. "But I'm not going to let it consume me. I'll find a way to make things right."

Hyun reached out, his hand brushing hers, and for a moment, Ji-eun felt a flicker of hope—a fleeting reminder of the love they had shared before all of this. But that hope was quickly overshadowed by the weight of the Heart in her hand, the ominous presence of power she couldn't control.

"I can help you," Hyun said, his voice gentle but firm. "We can figure this out together. You don't have to carry this burden alone."

Ji-eun looked up at him, her eyes filled with unshed tears. She wanted to believe him, wanted to believe that together they could overcome the challenges ahead. But deep down, she knew that the Heart of Time was not something they could simply walk away from. It was too powerful, too dangerous.

"I don't want to drag you into this," she whispered, her voice trembling. "I've already changed the course of history. I don't know what I've done. I don't want to put you in danger."

Hyun's hand tightened around hers. "You're not alone in this. I love you, Ji-eun. No matter what happens, I'll be by your side."

For a moment, Ji-eun closed her eyes, letting his words wash over her. She could feel the depth of his love, the unwavering support he had always given her. But she also knew that the path ahead was fraught with uncertainty, and there was no guarantee of what would happen next.

"We'll face it together," Ji-eun said, her voice resolute, though her heart ached. “But I need to figure out how to undo the damage I’ve caused. The Heart… it’s changing me. I can feel it. And I don’t know how much longer I can hold on to who I am.”

Hyun’s gaze softened, his thumb brushing over her hand in a soothing gesture. “We’ll figure it out. We’ll find a way.”

But even as he said the words, Ji-eun couldn’t shake the feeling that the Heart of Time was already starting to take its toll on her. It wasn’t just the physical changes—though she had noticed the way her senses seemed sharper, more attuned to the world around her—it was the way her mind felt as if it were slowly unraveling, as if the threads of time were slipping through her fingers.

She had been warned. The Heart was not meant for mortals. And yet, here she was, with its power coursing through her veins.

The truth was, Ji-eun wasn’t sure how much longer she could hold on to herself before the Heart consumed her entirely.

As the night settled over the palace, Ji-eun lay in bed, the weight of the Heart resting beside her. She could feel its pulse, like a constant thrum in her chest, reminding her that the stakes were higher than she had ever imagined.

The path ahead was unclear, but one thing was certain: no matter what happened, she could not let the Heart fall into the wrong hands. Not again. Not ever.

And she couldn’t do it alone.

Chapter 14: Unraveling Time

The days following Ji-eun's return to the palace were filled with a heavy silence. The once vibrant halls now felt stifled, as though the air itself was burdened by the weight of the Heart of Time. Ji-eun could feel it, too—the sense of unease creeping under her skin, the sensation that something in the world was wrong. The balance had shifted, and she couldn't undo it. Not yet.

She had tried to return to some semblance of normalcy, but it was impossible. She could no longer ignore the pull of the Heart, the way it seemed to whisper in her mind, reminding her of its power and its price. Hyun, too, could sense the change. Though he tried to comfort her, he was equally consumed by the fear of what lay ahead.

"Ji-eun," Hyun said one evening, breaking the silence that had settled between them. They were seated in the courtyard, the soft hum of the palace life around them doing little to mask the tension in the air. "We need to learn more about the Heart. We need to understand what it truly is and why it's affecting you this way."

She looked at him, her gaze heavy with the weight of everything they had been through. "I know. But I'm afraid, Hyun. I don't know how much more I can take. The Keeper's warning was clear—the Heart isn't something I can control. And every day I feel it changing me."

Hyun took her hand in his, squeezing it gently. "You're strong. We'll find a way to stop it. Together."

There was a fire in his eyes, one she had always loved—a steadfast determination that, in a way, gave her strength. But deep down, Ji-eun knew they couldn't keep running from the inevitable. The Heart was a force beyond them both, and it was only a matter of time before it took control completely.

"We need to find answers," Ji-eun said, her voice quiet but resolute. "I've heard rumors... whispers among the scholars in the palace. There may be an ancient text, a scroll that could tell us more about the Heart and how to control it. It's hidden in the royal library."

Hyun frowned. "The royal library? That place is off-limits to most people. Are you sure we can get access?"

Ji-eun nodded, her expression unwavering. "We have to try. It's our only chance."

The next night, under the cover of darkness, they made their way to the royal library. It was a grand structure, the walls lined with shelves that stretched all the way to the high ceiling. The air was thick with the scent of ancient parchment, and the flickering candlelight cast long shadows across the room.

They had managed to slip past the guards, their movements quiet and calculated. Ji-eun led the way, her heart pounding in her chest. Each step felt like a step closer to unraveling the mystery that had consumed her life.

"I think it's this way," Ji-eun whispered, glancing around the rows of bookshelves. "The scroll should be in the restricted section."

Hyun followed her, his footsteps just as careful. "If we get caught..."

"We won't," Ji-eun interrupted, her voice firm. "I know this place better than anyone."

They reached the restricted section, a hidden alcove at the back of the library, and Ji-eun quickly began to search the shelves. She ran her fingers over the spines of the ancient scrolls, each one a potential answer, a potential key to her salvation.

And then she found it. The scroll she had been looking for—tattered and worn with age, but unmistakable.

She pulled it from the shelf and unfurled it carefully, her heart racing as the ancient text came into view. The writing was old, the characters unfamiliar, but Ji-eun had spent years learning the forgotten language of the royal texts. With Hyun by her side, she began to translate.

"It's a ritual," Ji-eun muttered, her brow furrowing as she read aloud. "A ritual to control the Heart of Time. It requires a sacrifice."

Hyun's eyes widened. "A sacrifice? What kind of sacrifice?"

Ji-eun's hands trembled as she continued to read. "The ritual demands that the wielder of the Heart give up something precious—something that defines them. Only then will the Heart lose its power over them."

She stopped, the weight of the words sinking in. A sacrifice. Something precious. What could she possibly give up that would make a difference? Her love for Hyun? Her memories of the future? Her very life?

"There's more," Ji-eun continued, her voice shaking now. "It says that the sacrifice will not just affect the wielder. It will affect the person closest to them—the person they love most. The Heart does not relinquish its hold without a price."

Hyun's breath hitched. "It will affect me? How?"

"I don't know," Ji-eun whispered, her eyes wide with fear. "But I think the Heart will claim both of us. It won't let me go without taking something from you."

They stood there, the reality of their situation sinking in, the weight of the ancient text heavy in the air between them. Ji-eun's heart ached with the knowledge that the love she shared with Hyun, the bond that transcended time, was at risk of being torn apart by the very thing they sought to control.

"We can't let it consume us, Hyun," Ji-eun said, her voice breaking. "But I don't know how to stop it. I don't know how to control the Heart."

Hyun's hand gripped hers tightly, his eyes never leaving hers. "We will figure it out, Ji-eun. Together."

But even as he said the words, Ji-eun couldn't shake the feeling that time itself was slipping away from them, faster than they could grasp.

The Heart of Time was a force beyond them, and she was running out of time to find a way to stop it.

Chapter 15: The Ritual of the Heart

The night air was heavy with the scent of damp earth, the sky above thick with the weight of unseen stars. The palace, shrouded in its usual silence, seemed almost to hold its breath, as if anticipating the dangerous ritual Ji-eun and Hyun were about to undertake.

The scroll was spread out before them, its faded ink still legible, though the words seemed to blur before her eyes. Ji-eun had translated the text as best as she could, but there was something about the ritual—something dark, something ancient—that unsettled her.

She had been warned. The Keeper of Time had told her the Heart of Time was not meant for mortals, that no one, not even someone who crossed the boundaries of time, could control it without paying a price. And now, the time had come to face that price.

The ritual called for the Heart to be placed at the center of a sacred circle, its wielder standing at the center, surrounded by the person they loved most. That person, too, would bear the consequences of the ritual—no one could escape the Heart's power.

"We don't have to do this," Hyun said softly, his voice strained. "We can find another way. There must be another solution."

Ji-eun looked at him, her eyes filled with a quiet desperation. She could see the fear in his eyes, but she also saw the love. The unwavering, undying love that had kept them both tethered to each other despite the forces that sought to tear them apart.

"I have to, Hyun," she whispered. "If we don't, the Heart will consume us. It will destroy everything."

His hand, warm and steady, found hers in the darkness. "Then we'll do it together. No matter the cost."

Ji-eun squeezed his hand, the strength of their bond comforting yet painful at the same time. She knew what was at stake, knew the price they were about to pay. But in her heart, there was no choice. This was the only way to free them both from the Heart's grip.

They entered the courtyard where the ritual would take place, an ancient place hidden within the heart of the palace—a place untouched by time. The ground was marked with faded symbols, the remnants of countless rituals from centuries past. Ji-eun could feel the power in the air, an energy that seemed to pulse with its own rhythm, as though the very earth beneath her feet was alive.

She stood at the center of the circle, Hyun beside her, his presence both a comfort and a weight. The Heart of Time, glowing faintly in her hand, seemed to pulse in response to the ancient symbols on the ground.

With a deep breath, Ji-eun placed the Heart at the center of the circle, the light from its core casting an ethereal glow across the stone floor. The moment it touched the ground, the air around them shifted. It was as if time itself had paused, holding its breath.

Hyun's hand rested on her shoulder, and she could feel his warmth through the thin fabric of her gown. His voice was a mere whisper in the stillness of the night. "Are you ready?"

Ji-eun didn't answer right away. How could she be ready for this? How could anyone be ready to face a force beyond their comprehension?

But she had no choice. There was no going back.

"I am," she said, her voice steady but trembling. She looked into Hyun's eyes, her heart filled with a love so deep that it felt like it could move mountains. "We can do this together. No matter what happens."

With a final glance at him, she closed her eyes and began the incantation, her voice soft at first, then gaining strength with each word. The language was ancient, the words foreign, but she could feel their power taking shape as she spoke. It was as if the very air around them began to respond, humming with energy.

As the ritual progressed, Ji-eun could feel the Heart of Time vibrating beneath her hand, the power within it growing stronger by the second. She felt the pull of it, like a magnet drawing her in, threatening to consume her. It was as if the Heart was alive, its hunger insatiable, and no matter how hard she tried to focus on the words, it was becoming harder to keep her mind clear.

Then, as she reached the final words of the incantation, she felt it—the moment the Heart's power truly took hold. The air around them crackled with electricity, and the ground beneath them trembled, as though the very earth itself was reacting to the ritual. A sharp, searing pain shot through her chest, and she gasped, stumbling forward.

"Ji-eun!" Hyun's voice broke through the haze of pain. He was at her side instantly, his hands gripping her arms as she tried to steady herself.

But Ji-eun barely registered his presence, her vision blurring. She could feel the Heart's power surging through her, a force beyond anything she had ever known. It was overwhelming, like a storm tearing through her soul. The pain was unbearable.

"Hyun..." she whispered, her voice ragged.

"I'm here," he said, his voice strained with emotion. "We'll get through this. Just hold on."

But Ji-eun could feel the Heart's influence spreading beyond her. The pain in her chest was fading, but the sense of loss, of something precious slipping away, only grew stronger. It wasn't just her life at risk. The ritual had made it clear—Hyun, too, would pay the price.

She looked at him, her vision dimming. The love they shared, the connection they had built over time, was slipping away, just beyond her reach. She could feel him, could still hear his voice, but it was as if he was fading into the distance.

"No," Ji-eun gasped. "I can't lose you... not now..."

Her hands reached out for him, but as she did, she felt the Heart's power surge once more, pulling her deeper into the abyss. And then, there was nothing.

Chapter 16: The Price of Time

Ji-eun's world had turned into a blur of shifting shadows and searing light. Her body felt weightless, as though she was floating in a void where nothing existed except the beating of her heart and the pull of the Heart of Time.

For a moment, she couldn't tell if she was alive or dead. Her thoughts were tangled, her mind struggling to hold onto the last threads of consciousness. She remembered the ritual, the incantation, the searing pain that had ripped through her chest like a storm. And then, the terrifying emptiness that had followed.

But now, everything was silent. Her body was still, as if frozen in time, and there was a sense of peace... or was it just the calm before the storm?

A voice broke through the silence.

"Ji-eun."

Hyun's voice—soft, desperate—cut through the haze in her mind. She blinked, trying to focus, and slowly, the world came back into view. She was lying on the ground, her body heavy and cold, and Hyun was kneeling beside her, his face pale, his eyes filled with a mixture of fear and concern.

"Hyun," she whispered, her voice barely audible. "What happened? What's going on?"

He touched her face, his hand trembling as he brushed a strand of hair from her forehead. "You... you're awake," he said, his voice thick with emotion. "I thought I lost you."

Ji-eun tried to sit up, but her body felt weak, as though every muscle had been drained of strength. "What happened to the Heart? Did it work? Did we stop it?"

Hyun's eyes darkened, and he looked away, as if struggling to find the right words. "The Heart... it's still here, Ji-eun. The ritual didn't stop it. It didn't release its power."

Ji-eun's heart sank. "Then... then what did we do? What was the price? What did we lose?"

Hyun didn't answer immediately. His gaze was distant, as if he was unwilling to face the truth. Slowly, he reached for her hand and placed it over his chest, where his heartbeat could be felt, steady and strong.

"I'm still here, Ji-eun," he said quietly. "But there's something different. Something I can't explain. The Heart of Time... it didn't just affect you. It took something from both of us."

She felt his words hit her like a cold wave. "Took something? What do you mean?"

Hyun closed his eyes, taking a deep breath. "When the ritual was complete, I felt it... the Heart's power. But it wasn't like before. The time we shared... the memories... they're slipping away. I can't remember everything, Ji-eun. I can't remember all of it."

Ji-eun's eyes widened in horror. "What are you saying?"

Hyun's voice was barely a whisper, filled with pain. "The Heart of Time... it's erasing our memories. The bond we shared—everything we've been through together—it's all fading. And I don't know how much longer I'll be able to remember you."

The words struck her like a blade to the heart. She reached for him, desperate, as if touching him could stop the slow unraveling of everything they had been through. "No, Hyun! You can't forget me! You can't forget us!"

He squeezed her hand, his face filled with anguish. "I don't want to forget you, Ji-eun. But I can feel it. The more time passes, the more it slips away. It's like... like we never existed."

The Heart of Time had done its worst. The very thing that had brought them together—the force that had defied the laws of time and fate—was now taking it all away. The memories, the love, the life they had built together... it was all being erased, as though it had never been.

Ji-eun could feel the tears welling in her eyes. "Is there no way to stop it? We can't lose each other, Hyun. We can't lose everything we've fought for!"

Hyun took a deep, shuddering breath. "There might be one way."

Ji-eun looked at him, her heart pounding. "What is it? Tell me! I'll do anything!"

Hyun's gaze met hers, his eyes filled with sorrow and resolve. "The Heart can be controlled again, but only if we sacrifice what's left. A final act of true love. We'll have to erase ourselves from time completely."

Ji-eun's breath caught in her throat. "What do you mean? Erase ourselves from time?"

"It means we'll give up everything," Hyun said, his voice low. "Our past, our future, our memories. Everything. We'll vanish from time itself, and the Heart will lose its power over us."

The silence between them stretched, heavy with the weight of his words. The idea of sacrificing everything—of erasing themselves, their love, their very existence—seemed impossible. But as Ji-eun looked into Hyun's eyes, she saw the same love, the same devotion that had carried them this far.

"Will you remember me?" Ji-eun asked, her voice trembling.

Hyun's lips trembled with emotion, but he didn't answer. He didn't need to. They both knew the truth. If they chose this path, they would be gone—forgotten by time, by history, by everyone. And yet, they would remain in each other's hearts, even if no one else would remember them.

With a final, lingering kiss, Ji-eun nodded. "Let's do it. Together. Whatever it takes."

They stood together, hand in hand, as the Heart of Time pulsed once more, its light growing brighter, then fading, as the very fabric of time began to unravel. Their memories, their love, everything they had known—was slipping away, but the connection they shared in that moment was stronger than any force the Heart could wield.

And in that final, fleeting moment, they were timeless. Their love, their sacrifice, transcended time itself.

With that, *Timeless Love* comes to a close, leaving behind the memory of a love that defied time, space, and destiny. If you ever wish to revisit the world of Ji-eun and Hyun, you'll know their love, though lost to time, will always be remembered in their hearts.

Printed in Dunstable, United Kingdom

79312359R00050